P9-CAL-671

Written by Frank B. Edwards
Illustrated by John Bianchi

First published in 1997 by Bungalo Books.)

Cataloguing in Publication Data

Edwards, Frank B., 1952-
Peek-a-boo at the zoo

(Pokeweed Press new reader series)

ISBN 1-894323-06-8 (pbk.)

I. Bianchi, John II. Title. III. Series.

PS8559.D84P43 1999 jC813'.54 C99-900265-1
PZ7.E2535Pe 1999

Published in North America by:
Pokeweed Press
17 Elk Court, Suite 200
Kingston, Ontario
K7M 7A4

Visit Pokeweed Press on the Net at:
www.Pokeweed.com

Send E-mail to Pokeweed Press at:
publisher@pokeweed.com

Printed in Canada by:
Friesens Corporation

American sales and marketing by:
Stoddart Kids
a division of Stoddart Publishing Co. Ltd.
180 Varick Street, 9th Floor
New York, New York 10014

Canadian sales and marketing by:
General Publishing
34 Lesmill Road
Toronto, ON
M3B 2T6

Visit General Publishing on the Net at:
www.genpub.com

Distributed in the U.S.A. by:
General Distribution Services
Suite 202
85 River Rock Drive
Buffalo, NY 14207

Distributed in Canada by:
General Distribution Services
325 Humber College Blvd.
Toronto, ON
M9W 7C3

Peek-a-boo at the Zoo

Written by Frank B. Edwards
Illustrated by John Bianchi

passenger
bus
tree
log
bush
pond
rock

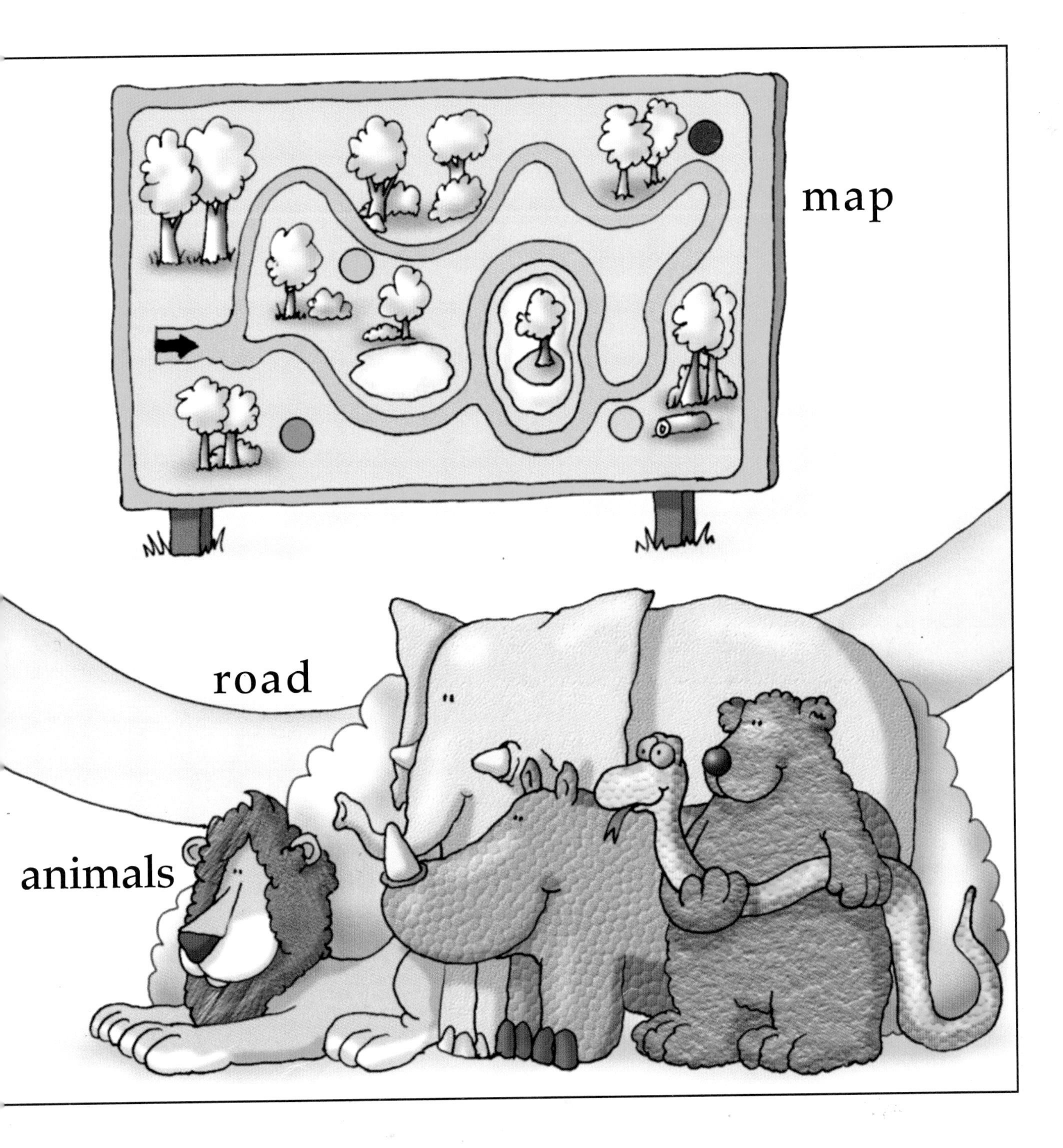
map
road
animals

Peek-a-boo. Where are you?

Monkey

Look again. I am here

Monkey

Peek-a-boo. Where are you?

Lion
Tiger

Look again. We are here.

Peek-a-boo. Where are you?

Snake
Giraffe
Ostrich

Look again. We are here.

Peek-a-boo. Where are you?

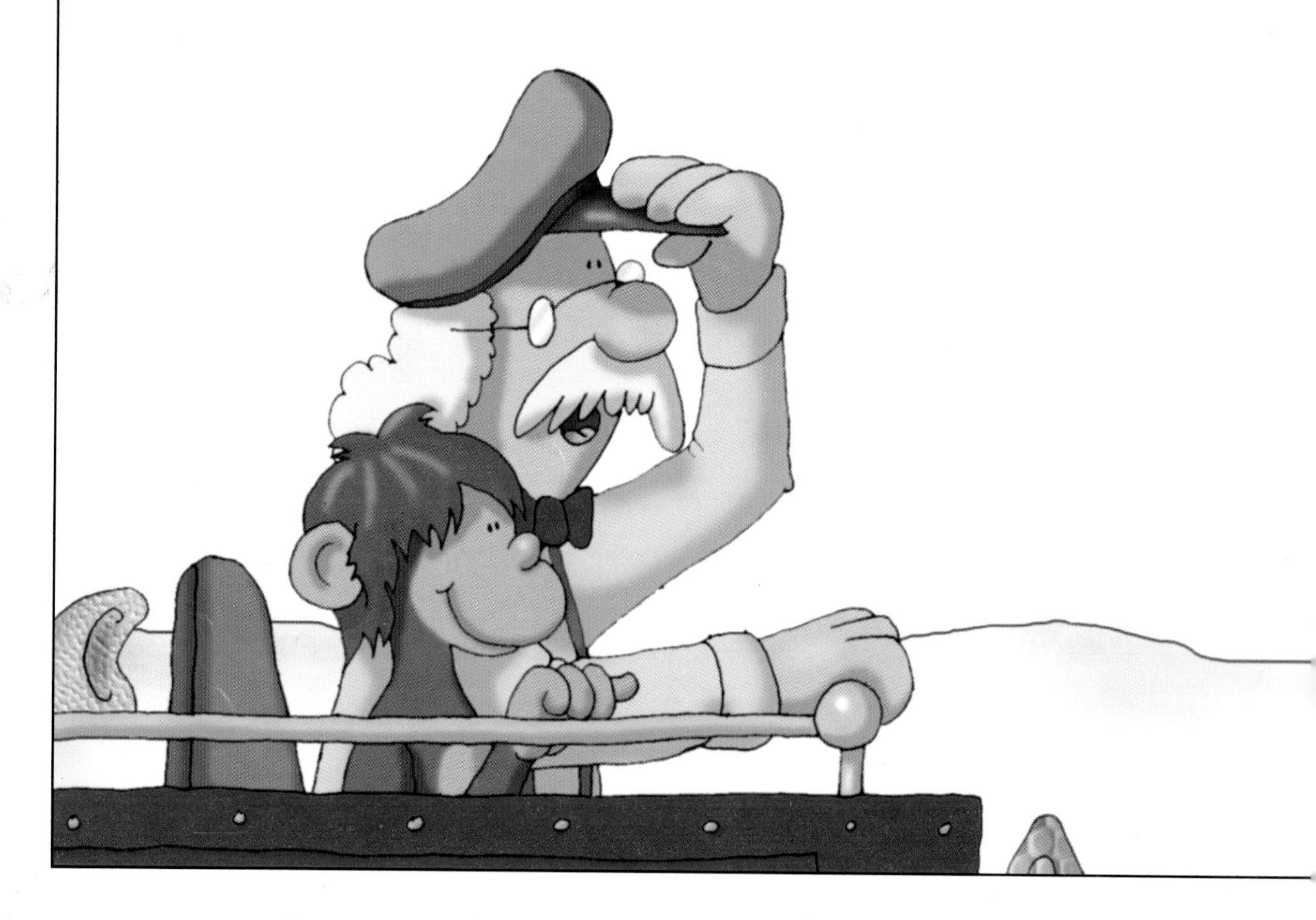

Bear
Bird
Rhinoceros
Elephant

Look again. We are here.

Now where did you all go?

Look around.
We are all in here!

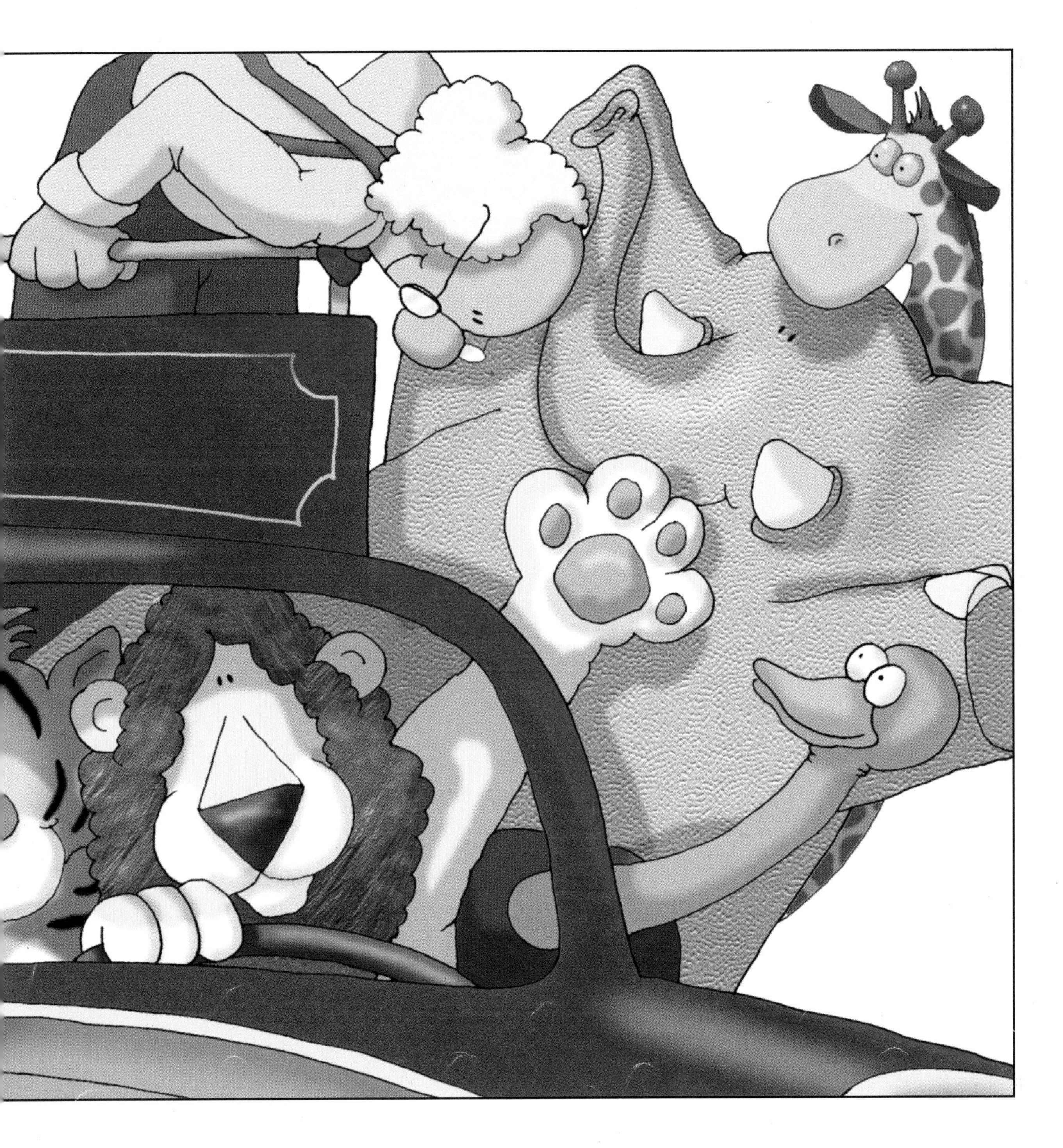

The End